W9-BAQ-420

THE NIGHT BEFORE
CHRISTMAS

By Clement C. Moore

Illustrated by Corinne Malvern

A GOLDEN BOOK • NEW YORK
Western Publishing Company, Inc., Racine, Wisconsin 53404

*This Christmas favorite was written in 1822
by Clement C. Moore for his own children. He later
published it as A VISIT FROM ST. NICHOLAS.
Dr. Moore taught Biblical history in New York City.
In the neighborhood where the poem was written,
an annual Christmas party is given. At this
party some well-known person reads*
THE NIGHT BEFORE CHRISTMAS.

Copyright 1949 by Western Publishing Company, Inc. Copyright renewed 1977. All rights
reserved. Printed in the U.S.A. No part of this book may be reproduced or copied in any form
without written permission from the publisher. GOLDEN®, GOLDEN & DESIGN®, A
LITTLE GOLDEN BOOK® and A GOLDEN BOOK® are trademarks of Western Publishing
Company, Inc. ISBN 0-307-02068-1

DECEMBER 1822

SUN	MON	TUE	WED	THU	FRI	SAT
1	2	3	4	5	6	7
8	9	10	11	12	13	14
15	16	17	18	19	20	21
22	23	24	25	26	27	28
29	30	31				

'Twas the night before Christmas when all
through the house
Not a creature was stirring, not even a mouse.

The stockings were hung by the chimney with care,
In hopes that Saint Nicholas soon would be there.

The children were nestled all snug in their beds,
While visions of sugarplums danced in their heads,

And Mamma in her kerchief and I in my cap,
Had just settled down for a long winter's nap.
When out on the lawn there arose such a clatter,

I sprang from my bed to see what was the matter.
Away to the window I flew like a flash,
Tore open the shutters and threw up the sash.

The moon on the breast of the new-fallen snow
Gave a luster of midday to objects below,
When, what to my wondering eyes should appear,
But a miniature sleigh, and eight tiny reindeer;

With a little old driver, so lively and quick,
I knew in a moment it must be St. Nick.

More rapid than eagles his coursers they came.
And he whistled, and shouted, and called them
    by name:
"Now, Dasher! now, Dancer! now, Prancer
    and Vixen!
On, Comet! on, Cupid! on, Donner and Blitzen!
To the top of the porch, to the top of the wall!
Now, dash away, dash away, dash away all!"

As dry leaves that before the wild hurricane fly,
When they meet with an obstacle, mount to the sky,

So up to the house-top the coursers they flew
With a sleigh full of toys, and St. Nicholas, too.

And then in a twinkle, I heard on the roof
The prancing and pawing of each little hoof.
As I drew in my head, and was turning around,
Down the chimney St. Nicholas came with a bound.

He was dressed all in fur, from his head to his foot,
And his clothes were all tarnished with ashes and soot;
A bundle of toys he had flung on his back,
And he looked like a peddler just opening his pack.

His eyes how they twinkled! his dimples how merry!
His cheeks were like roses, his nose like a cherry.
His droll little mouth was drawn up like a bow,
And the beard on his chin was as white as the snow.

The stump of a pipe he held tight in his teeth,
And the smoke, it encircled his head like a wreath.
He had a broad face and a little round belly
That shook, when he laughed, like a bowl full of jelly.

He was chubby and plump, a right jolly old elf.
And I laughed when I saw him, in spite of myself.

A wink of his eye, and a twist of his head,
Soon gave me to know I had nothing to dread;

He spoke not a word, but went straight to his work,
And filled all the stockings; then turned with a jerk,

And laying his finger aside of his nose,
And giving a nod, up the chimney he rose.

He sprang to his sleigh, to his team gave a whistle,
And away they all flew like the down on a thistle.

But I heard him exclaim as he drove out of sight,

"Happy Christmas to all and to all a good night."